Al

Ahlam Bsharat is a Palestinian writer who grew up in a village in Northern Palestine. She completed her Master's Degree in Arabic Literature at An-Najah National University in Nablus. Besides poetry, picture books, short stories, novels and memoirs, she has written a number of television and radio scripts. Her books have received many awards and recommendations. *Ismee Alharakee Farasha* (translated into English as *Code Name: Butterfly*) was included in the IBBY Honour List for 2012, a biennial selection of outstanding, recently published books from more than seventy countries. *Ismee Alharakee Farasha* and *Ashjaar lil-Naas al-Ghaa'ibeen* (translated into English as *Trees for the Absentees*) were both runners-up for the Etisalat Award For Arabic Children's Literature in 2013. *Code Name: Butterfly* was also shortlisted for the UK-based Palestine Book Awards in 2017.

Ahlam has been active in numerous cultural forums, and her craft has taken her to Belgium, France and Spain, where she was artist in residence. She has also led many creative writing workshops for children and adults, including at the Emirates Literature Festival in Dubai.

TREES *for the* ABSENTEES

Ahlam Bsharat

Translated from the Arabic
by Ruth Ahmedzai Kemp and Sue Copeland

NEEM TREE
PRESS

This is a work of fiction. Names, characters, businesses, places, events and incidents are either the products of the author's imagination or used in a fictitious manner. Any resemblance to actual persons, living or dead, or actual events is purely coincidental.

Neem Tree Press Limited, 1st Floor,
2 Woodberry Grove, London, N12 0DR, UK
Published by Neem Tree Press Limited 2019
info@neemtreepress.com

Originally published in Arabic as *Ashjaar lil-Naas al-Ghaa'ibeen*
by Tamer Institute 2013

Copyright © Ahlam Bsharat 2013
Translation Copyright © Ruth Ahmedzai Kemp
and Sue Copeland 2019

A catalogue record for this book is available from the British Library

ISBN 978-1-911107-23-1 (paperback)
ISBN 978-1-911107-24-8 (e-book)

All rights reserved. No part of this publication may be reproduced, distributed, or transmitted in any form or by any means, including photocopying, recording, or other electronic or mechanical methods, without the prior written permission of the publisher, except in the case of brief quotations embodied in critical reviews and certain other noncommercial uses permitted by copyright law.

For permission requests, write to the publisher at the address above.

Printed and bound in Great Britain
by Clays Ltd, Elcograf S.p.A.

"When they saw me, those are the eyes which gave me love."

Traditional song sung by Pashtun women

CONTENTS

1

The LIGHT

"Philistia! Philistia!"

The woman calling me was a regular at the hammam. Once a month without fail. She called my name in a full-bodied warble, like a singer warming up before a performance.

"You do have a funny name, Philistia," she told me. This wasn't the first time. She never tired of making this observation, apparently. She certainly didn't seem to notice that she was repeating herself.

I carried on scrubbing her arm, trying to ignore her comment. She started laughing out loud.

"Oh Philistia, you're making me giggle!"

Her laughter was muffled like voices under water. I could hear the sound and yet couldn't hear it properly. A chuckle echoing around this hall of laughter.

I pictured the hammam as a laughter market, and whenever a woman giggled it was as if a trader were setting up a stall and putting a new laugh out on display for customers to try – a *brand-spanking-new* one, as Grandma Zahia always used to say. A brand-spanking-new laugh, and alongside them, three roses as dark as wine, laid there randomly – because who would put them there on purpose? They had just appeared there somehow of their own volition. This seedling of a laugh and beside it some self-seeded roses that deep wine red, or perhaps four carnations: one white, one yellow and the other two the pink of fresh, cool watermelon flesh. Who knows what made me think of those particular garden flowers or that range of shades from the colour palette. But I never pictured roses in purple, for some reason. Is there even such a thing as a purple rose? My friend Fathia once said that violet was the colour of sadness. I didn't want to be sad.

The woman who visited the hammam once a month could just say, "You're making me giggle!" But no, she insisted on tagging on "Philistia", as she always did. She began or ended every single utterance with my name.

My palm scrubbed her upper arm with the exfoliating mitt, while my other hand poured water over it.

"No, no," she said with a coquettish giggle. "You haven't finished my armpit, Philistia." And again she added, "You do have a funny name, Philistia." She followed this with, "And your eyes are always wandering. They never fix on one place, Philistia."

I scrubbed her elbow. She looked like she was laid out on the bed in a doctor's surgery, not a spongy hammam mat.

"Philistia, I want to get rid of that awful dark patch. I've tried all kinds of prescriptions and ointments, but nothing makes a difference." She asked me about the colour of the elbows of the other women whose bodies I scrubbed and what creams they used. "Don't you hear what they use, Philistia? Don't you see the colour of their elbows, Philistia?"

No, I don't hear. I don't see. And I don't speak.

It wasn't hard for me to numb my senses. I'm used to seeing naked bodies; I have been since I was little. Grandma Zahia used to say, "Our heads are cupboards full of secrets, and our senses are the key. Everything that your eyes see becomes yours to keep safe. If you take something with you, then hide it away. Whatever they give you willingly, spread it out before you and wash it like you wash lentils, sieving out other bits of dirt. The body contains both bad and good, and all that is within the body belongs to it. When someone entrusts their body to you, they open the door to reveal their secrets. That's the time to close the door to your own cupboard of secrets."

So I had learned to close the doors and drawers of the cupboard in my head. I could open my senses and yet keep them slightly ajar. I could see women's bodies and yet not truly see them. What happened inside the hammam seemed to mirror what happened outside. The things I noticed out there were the same things I noticed in here, but here in the hammam everything was all so familiar that it became more dull and more ordinary. The monotony and repetition meant my senses adapted; things seemed normal here that wouldn't seem normal outside. A woman revealing her body to me – would she do that if we met at another place and another time, out there in the real world?

Sometimes the worlds merged in the cupboard of my mind: reality was my imagination and my imagination was reality. Like that woman I saw in the street once. Our eyes met, but she seemed to come from another world. It was outside the Arab Bank in the centre of Nablus. I saw her in the crowd and it was like I knew her from another place and another time. She was holding her ATM card in her hand and trying to put her purse back in her bag.

She seemed different, and yet there was something about her that was just like any other woman laid out in the hammam on the stone in front of me. So I put on my rough black hand mitt from Aleppo and started to scrub her body. She said to me, "I want to laugh. Rub the soles of my feet." So I scrubbed the soles of her feet, but she didn't laugh.

When I reached her chest, there were her breasts and she said something so softly that I couldn't make out what she said. All I could make out was that she muttered something, but I didn't hear what. My eyes focused on seeing and I read her body. I took her first breast and I scrubbed it. I took her second breast and I scrubbed it. She closed her eyes and her lips were the shape of a smile broken into two halves. Thinking about it again, it wasn't the same woman who lay before me now: hers was a whole mouth, her lips pursed with worry.

Grandma Zahia used to bring babies into this world, dragging them out by their heads, by their feet, taking them by the hand as they crossed from that other world into ours. How did they feel later? When day by day they found themselves in a hostile, unknown world, a disappointing one. When they discovered that the transition from darkness to light was not what it was made out to be. Did they thank Grandma? Had she saved them when she brought them into life, or had she deceived them?

I asked Grandma Zahia once but she said nothing. I was playing hopscotch in front of the house. I was getting annoyed, trying to get a bit of rock embedded in the ground to lie flat. "Help me, Grandma!" I said.

I balanced on one leg by a piece of flat rock, my hand resting on her head as she scraped away at the soil with her fingers, insisting on levelling out the ground as though she were the one who was going to play. I said, "You're deceiving the people of the village of Deir Sabra, Grandma! You're filling the world with children who are lost."

As Grandma carried on scraping away, I added, "You're making space for this rock," and I shook my hand holding the stone, not taking my eyes off it. "Fine! That's easy. But maybe you're setting it up for me to trip over it. I'll get up, because you're here to hold my hand. But what about those newborn babies with their tender flesh? You're not there to help them."

Grandma kept on working away at the soil, while I ranted on. "You're deceiving them, Grandma! Well, I'm not having anything more to do with it! Take that!" I threw the rock on the ground and I ran.

I ran and ran, and all I could think of was Dad, who hadn't let us visit him for over a year. I ran and ran until I reached the shady spot under the big tree on top of the hill, and the image of Dad became clearer and clearer, although my eyes were blurry with tears. I leaned back against the huge tree trunk and closed my eyes. I pictured brand-new babies, with ruddy cheeks and on their backs ornate wings, which folded at their sides. Their wings fluttered as they descended from heaven. They were like plump birds spreading their wings and laughing. They each carried a burning torch.

When Grandma caught up with me, I whispered it all to her as we sat beneath the tree in the shade. She hugged me to her chest and I felt the two inflatable balls squashed under her robe, her gold necklace clinking as she moved.

"What you saw was real," she said, stroking my hair with her hand. "We are all visitors on this earth.

We all arrive carrying our flame with us. There are those who use that flame to light up the darkness, and there are those who use it to set fire to trees and people. Deceiving people, my sweet, would be how we *use* our flame in life, not how we bring it into life. I open up the path for that light. I grab hold of a foot and pull the baby towards the darkness of life for him to light it up. And you are a helping hand to help me as I tug this light into our world."

That night I dreamed that Grandma Zahia and I were dragging along a heavy lamp. We couldn't rest even for a short moment, in case it got away. We walked and walked, surrounded by a huge pool of light, as big as the canopy of the shady tree, and the world was like a gleaming sphere around us.

I wrote to Dad and told him about the bird-babies. About the heavy lamp we were dragging along. About Grandma Zahia who pulled the light into our world with every baby she delivered. About how I helped her pull. About the women's bodies and how my hand moved in the field of their magnetic light. I confessed to him how afraid I am of being left as a single light all alone. And I reassured him that although he wasn't here, his light was still with me. Sometimes it faded, but it never went out.

And I asked him about it: "Dad, where do you hide your light, to keep it safe?"

The other day, my boss at the hammam, Umm Walid, asked me, "Why do you leave your hand lingering on the women's bodies? Like your arm's dangling from the ceiling?"

"I'm trying to understand their secrets," I replied. "My hand is drawn to their light."

"You're a mysterious one, Philistia," said Umm Walid. "But the good thing is I've had no complaints about you."

"No one complains if someone helps them carry their light."

Do you know what, Dad? We spend this life looking for someone to help us carry our light. I'm sure when you proposed to Mum, you must have asked her, "Najwa, will you let me help you carry your light?" And I'm sure she said yes. Otherwise how did I come into this world? And Nahil, Sawsan and Saeed? Four little cherubs each carrying a flaming torch and running with it!

2

The CAT'S *got my* TONGUE

I barely slept that night from worrying. I was anxious all night and even more so as daybreak approached. I got out from under the covers and tiptoed around the room. I thought about opening the window and looking out at the autumn sky, but I didn't. I was afraid the uncaring wind would blow in a leaf from its mother's bough and I would catch it in my hands, and what would I do with a dead leaf in my hands? Grandma Zahia hadn't taught me to wash dead leaves!

"It's fine," Auntie Hoda had said earlier that day, as she secured the nappy over her baby's tawny thighs. "There's no shame in work."

Auntie Mariam, who lived nearby, disagreed. "There most certainly IS! I bear responsibility for her! How can I live with the shame? My brother's daughter working in a place where women strip off and expose themselves to each other!"

"The brother you are talking about," Mum interjected, "has been in prison for five years and we still haven't seen a single penny from you!"

Auntie Mariam laughed mischievously as she put her cup of tea down on the table and got up to leave. "You think you and your daughter aren't getting your dues? You're getting my brother's benefits from the Ministry for Prisoners, not to mention the charity that falls into your lap while you sit around at home. There are many hands ready to help … but I suppose a leopard never changes its spots."

I broke into the conversation. "Auntie, this job is something *I* want to do – not Mum!"

My aunt ignored me, as if I were speaking in sign language behind her back, gesturing in a silent cartoon. I suspected her leopard comment was a dig at Grandma Zahia, which clearly annoyed Mum. When my aunt left the room, Mum slammed the door after her.

My younger siblings carried on playing, entirely indifferent to this conversation, which didn't concern them, after all. Saeed was pushing his train along the floor, stopping every now and then for a "choo choo" to emerge – from his mouth, obviously, not from the train. No black smoke came out of Saeed's mouth or from his stupid train. It was nothing like a real train, which neither of us had ever seen in real life, only once or twice on the television.

Sawsan was combing her doll's hair and nodding to a silent rhythm. I don't know why – I suppose she was dancing to a drumbeat in her head. Nahil was standing at the bathroom door, wrapping her hair in a towel and singing a Nancy Ajram song. "What's on your mind, *habibi*, and why don't you speak to me?"

But that was the day before. The next morning Mum and I were crossing the road to catch the minibus. The city was crowded with people. I was tense and getting more so. Everyone around me – all these strangers – they all seemed to know where they were going. Even Mum was like a stranger who knew her way. That thing happened to me that can happen even with the people closest to us when you find yourself in a strange place. An unfamiliar place, a new context and the relationship suddenly feels completely different.

"Honestly, it does happen," I once told Fathia. "When I see my father behind bars it's like it's a portrait of a man in prison, and we have some kind of connection to him but it's not clear what it is. Is the connection just the act of visiting him now and then? As far as he's concerned, we're just people who come and see him, some young people and a woman called 'children' and 'wife'. And then what? When he gets out, and he comes over to play with us and we play with him, will our relationship still be based on the verb 'to visit'? Then our house will become a prison too."

My mum also once said, "Abu Mansur never left the house again after he was released from prison. His house became his prison."

Mum and I were linked in that moment by a connection based on the verb 'to walk'. It felt like we were two women walking along side by side without knowing why. True, my mum was maintaining a certain distance between us and, whenever we were separated by any further, she would look sideways or behind her to check I hadn't got lost, but I felt as though she was just a woman trying to take me somewhere safely, as though all that was going on in her mind was "When will I be able to get rid of her?"

A woman is like a guide in the desert. This was Mum's role in the desert of the city. And I? Was I the stubborn camel that had chosen its destination and headed deep into the desert? It seemed like I had strayed much further than I should have.

I remembered Mum's reaction the first time I broached the idea of looking for work.

"If you won't let me get my own job, I don't know why you ever let me go to work with Grandma Zahia," I huffed.

"What's Grandma Zahia got to do with it?" Mum shouted back. "Do you have to bring Grandma Zahia into it every time something doesn't work out as you want?"

"She does have something to do with it, Mum! Do you know why? Because finally the day has come when Philistia will no longer be blind."

Fear entered her voice. "Blind? Who said anything about being blind? God forbid!"

"Mum, I want to work," I said, as persuasively as I could. "I want to find a job for two or three days a week. Studying at Al-Quds Open University means it's flexible – I don't need to go there every day."

Mum had been as displeased about the idea of me studying at Al-Quds Open University as she was now about the idea of me getting a job. She had wanted me to enrol at An-Najah, the largest university in Palestine, like my cousin, so I could come home at the same time as her and ideally dress the same as her and have the same handbag – though perhaps in a different colour or shoes with higher heels. Just to prove that I had a father who spent money on me like Auntie Mariam's daughter. It occurred to me then that mothers also have their reasons for acting like stroppy teenagers. Sometimes I felt like I had a mother who acted like my daughter, and a father to whom I wrote as if he were a distant penfriend I could not visit, in a context where it wasn't even easy to have a friendship between someone male and someone female in the first place.

This was my mum leading me across the city! Mum and me, her daughter, somehow or other playing our roles as expertly as we could. This was the tension that had built up over a night of worrying, of tossing and turning on my pillow, mounting fear and anxiety leaving me breathless.

I thought of screaming, "I want to go back! I've changed my mind!"

In that second I realised that everything that Auntie Mariam had said was a genuine attempt by a loving aunt to protect me – her brother's teenage daughter – from making a decision that betrayed my lack of experience. And Mum? It seemed to me she was motivated by the desire to resist my auntie's constant meddling in her life, especially since Dad was sent to prison. It made her feel obliged to support me in my decision. Forced to let me go, she was all of a sudden ready to throw me to an unknown fate among people I didn't know in a huge, strange city. I had almost completely lost confidence in my decision. After all, for all my attempts to show how grown-up I was, I was just a girl with no idea about life who woke up one day and said, "I will carry my own light!"

And now there was no choice but to become lost in this great harsh city, even though I still wanted to hang on to the hem of Mum's dress or cling to her neck. On my way back home I wouldn't have her dress or her neck to cling on to. When we got there, she was going to leave me and go.

Mum continued on her way. She crossed with me from one street to another amid strangers walking in a hurry, some of them smiling and laughing, others cheerless and gloomy. Were those gloomy ones going somewhere new and strange like me? Where they might become an easy morsel in the mouth of a fate they knew nothing about? I imagined they were heading to the hammam like me, and I wouldn't have been surprised if I found that some of them had arrived there before me and had already begun their work of scrubbing naked, unresisting bodies.

I thought, "Nablus, what a heartless city you are!" A place you don't know, I thought, is no different from a dead creature: grotesque and putrid with a smell that carries a reminder of all your old fears.

Mum gripped me by the hand and stepped on to the minibus. My feet followed hers. She asked a girl with wild hair flowing down her back about the fare. Her hand reached for her purse from the bag I was carrying for her. Mum tapped on the driver's shoulder and dropped the shekels into his hand. And from time to time she reminded him where we wanted to get off: "As close as possible to the market."

Black thoughts were battling in my head as the bus passed landscapes on both sides of a long road that I wished would never end. When Mum squeezed my hand, I felt it shatter like glass, shards of my hand penetrating into her flesh.

Should I say to Fathia, "Damn it, I wish you hadn't seen that advert and told me about it!" But wasn't I the one who had asked her to look for a job for me?

I remembered how she had knocked on the door that evening and pulled me by the hand into the kitchen, whispering, "I've found a job for you. Read the ad. It's perfect for you!" She went on, "And I think your Grandma Zahia is the one who sent it to you from up there." Fathia gestured upwards with her head as she said that, her eyes looking up as though she were searching for someone on the kitchen ceiling.

She smiled as she said it, but I was worried Mum would overhear her talking so loudly. "Shhh, Fathia, for goodness' sake!" I said, putting my hand over her mouth.

"Now, you're going to show me how clever you are," said Mum encouragingly, bringing me round from my thoughts. We had arrived. When I asked her how I would get back, she added, "He who asks for help never loses his way."

I walked behind her as we went through the door of the hammam then up three steps. I tugged her shoulder for her to wait for me, but she didn't turn to face me, she just stopped. The young man who was sitting behind the wooden screen at the entrance peered at me. He observed Mum's silence and he observed my hand on her arm as I pulled her gently to my side. My feeling of being lost seemed inescapable that autumn morning. But wasn't that what I had wanted?

"Rest assured," Mum said to the manager Umm Walid, patting her shoulder as they came to the end of a long conversation. "My daughter can be trusted to keep her mouth shut."

"She's quiet, isn't she?" commented Umm Walid. "Has the cat got her tongue?" Umm Walid seemed to be looking for a light-hearted parting comment with which to end her conversation with my mum, so she could get back to work.

Mum laughed, but I hid behind her back. How did Umm Walid know what everyone had said about me my whole life? Ever since I was a little girl, whether it was at home, at school or with my friends, I'd always been teased for being so quiet and they'd say the cat had got my tongue. When we studied idioms in Year 10, I realised it was the perfect example of a descriptive metaphor: the image of someone who says very little, who doesn't feel the desire to respond to everything that's going on around them or even what's being addressed to them.

"She's a girl of few words," Mum confirmed, "and she's a model of discretion. She can turn a blind eye – a skill she inherited from her Grandma Zahia."

Mum was a smooth talker like Fathia and every bit as good at selecting her words and steering the conversation. Mentioning my grandma gave Mum the opportunity to start telling Umm Walid about Grandma Zahia's historical role in the life of our village, about how she had been responsible for washing all the women and babies – the women when they passed from this world and the newborns when they entered it – for many long years, before she herself passed into the merciful embrace of Allah at the age of eighty-seven. Yet she had not found anyone to carry on her role and there was no one to wash her own corpse, except her fourteen-year-old granddaughter Philistia, who had boldly stepped up to the task amid a torrent of prayers for the soul of the deceased from female relatives, young and old, beseeching God to protect her in the afterlife, just as she had protected their loved ones in this world.

I still remember how the women watched me that day, saying, "*Masha'allah*, what a strong heart she has! Stronger than her mother. Look at her mother's hands trembling!"

"Look at her aunt!" they added. "Crying like a baby, hanging her head between her shoulders."

Her hands shaking, Mum moved the water jug around directly over my hands to spread the water over Grandma's body. Her skin was soft and it seemed as if green veins were trying to sprout up through it. She was no different in her dead body from how she was when she was alive. She seemed like a sleeping grandmother surrounded by rowdy children who ought to lower their voices, so they don't wake her up.

I imagined that everything I was doing was a role assigned to me in a recurring dream that constantly came to me in my sleep. Ever since Grandma Zahia had begun to take me with her round the houses to wash a woman who'd died, or a newborn child freshly emerged into life, I had begun to dream almost every day of naked flesh, stretched out, and of me pouring water on to the body from a metal jug. And as time went by, the water flowing from the spout of the jug transformed into a cascading waterfall or a spring where water dripped from a crack in the rock, like tears emerging between the eyelashes of a closed eye. I started to dream of old women dancing with newborn babies in the cascading water, all naked. And my task, together with

Grandma Zahia, was to oversee this ritual dance of babies and grown women.

And as an acknowledgement that no one can refute, Mum added, "For seventy years, it was in Grandma Zahia's hands that the people of Deir Sabra made the transitions of fate, passing into life or from life to death, and this is what every member of the village will testify about her. But what the people of Deir Sabra might have forgotten is that it was her granddaughter Philistia who assisted her when her own fate led her from life into death."

3

The REAL WORLD *and the* IMAGINARY WORLD

As time went by, I discovered that what happened in the hammam, where it was my job to bathe the living, was no different from what used to happen in the room where we washed the dead. If I can turn living people into corpses, then what's to stop me from bringing corpses back to life? They are our loved ones, as Grandma Zahia used to say, and we mustn't lose hope in their continued existence and their everlasting presence, even if they depart from us physically and no longer share our life.

And what did that have to do with my job at the hammam where I washed women who came to escape from their depression or grief? Or to make themselves beautiful for their husbands? Or get ready for their wedding? Or recover from a miscarriage? Or just to relax? These were women who came to the bath house to start a new chapter in their lives, each of them whispering in secret to themselves:

"I won't be as depressed after the hammam."

"I'll be so much more beautiful after the hammam!"

"I won't be a spinster after the hammam, I'll be married!"

"I was happy before the hammam and I will be afterwards, but somehow life will have a touch of something new."

"You ought to ask for a rise, Philistia," said my friend Fatima after I had been working there a little while. She smiled, her hands covered in soap lather from washing up. "You're the best thing that's happened to that hammam! And you should use some of your wages to remember your Grandma Zahia. You could give some to charity in her name, for the sake of her soul, because she's the one to thank for everything you know."

I smiled at that nice idea.

"Charity? Hmm. You know what they say – some eat chicken, while others sicken," chipped in Safa, who was flicking through a book, her legs dangling from the sofa that was covered with a flowery sheet with a rip in it.

"What are you two on about?" snapped Fathia, as she tied her hair up in a high ponytail. "You don't know anything about money or about Philistia! You've got someone to pay your college fees, Little Miss Chicken Licken, but Philistia here has to work to cover her fees, not to mention supporting her little brother and sister chicks, and fitting in visits to see her rooster dad in his prison coop in Ashkelon – if she's lucky and gets a travel permit from the Israeli hyenas, that is!"

My friends all laughed and so did I.

"Oh great, now we're on the funny farm!" Fatima joked.

Safa laughed, then explained, "I just meant that there are people here who don't give a stuff about what's going on around them and only care about themselves."

"I could strangle you, Miss Know-It-All!" Fathia burst out, reaching for Safa's neck. "You think God has given you and you alone the gift of sight!"

Safa jumped up from where she was sitting and started wrestling with Fathia. "I am a Know-It-All. Nothing happens without my knowledge. I know everything that goes on here – every little detail. Do you deny it?"

Now Fatima joined in. She put down the dish she had been washing and came up to Safa and Fathia, her hands covered in soap bubbles, and wiped them on their hair. "I'm the stupid one who doesn't know anything. The village idiot. And if you find out stuff I don't know about, don't tell me! I'm perfectly happy with my blissful ignorance."

The three of them were like hens pecking each other in the dirt, a blur of dappled brown and white feathers. Fathia dragged me by the hand and thrust me into the fray.

"We're at the hammam," she shouted. "And this is the Nabulsi soap!" She smeared suds on Fatima's hands then held her hands up to me, still heaped with bubbles. "Look!" she said. "Bathe us!" she commanded, grabbing my hands.

"I'll scrub your backs, your necks, your hair," I said, wiping my soapy hands on each of their backs in turn.

So, I ran my hands over their backs, their necks and their hair.

We pranced around, giggling. They each started barking orders like a military drill ("At ease … Attention!"), pointing to bits of their bodies for me to scrub: foot, chest, eyebrow, hair, bottom. We got sillier and sillier, and there was no shutting us up now, as we went on to shouting out the names of people, and abstract ideas, and political slogans. Tears, joy, intelligence, love, hate. Subhi is Fatima's beloved. Amir has eyes like honey. "Four-eyes" – the university professor with prescription glasses. The poet who makes all the girls go wild. Fathia's favourite writer – the one with the weekly column in *Al-Ayyam*. Ali who inspired Fathia to write poetry. The political posters and slogans. "Time to Elect A New National Council!" … "Yes to Unity, No to Division!" … "Yes to the Arab Spring!"… "Yes to Summer in Sharm el-Sheikh!" … "Arab Palestine, Islamic Palestine, International Palestine" … The supporters of Hamas, of Fatah, of the Popular Front, the Abu-Musab al-Zarqawi lot, the Bin Laden gang … all the factions, the splits … the splits on high, the split between your thighs …

"All right – that's enough about between your thighs!" wheezed Fatima, gasping in between laughs.

"Gently when you scrub down there!" screeched Fathia, wagging her finger in the air.

And we rolled about on the ground like cockroaches sprayed with Pif Paf, waving our legs in the air, clutching our stomachs. Safa's pale face was flushed red and Fathia was almost crying with laughter.

The Nablus night is not so different from the night in Deir Sabra, though there's something about it that is desolate and unsettling in its own way.

I wanted to stay over with Fathia in Nablus, but I still hadn't persuaded my mum to let me. How had Fathia managed to get her parents to let her stay there on her own?

"All the girls rent a room or a flat and stay over," Fathia had told her mum. "What's the problem?" And when that didn't work, she tried a different tack. "I'm going to be spending four years on the road between Deir Sabra and Nablus, Mum. You know it takes an hour each way because of the checkpoints, even though it's so close! When am I going to study?"

And when that didn't work, she shouted and stormed off. She went on hunger strike and eventually her parents caved in, and she ended up getting a place to stay in the city. A two-room flat on the fourth floor, with a bathroom, a kitchen and a balcony overlooking Al-Junaid prison.

"Look, you can see the prisoners pacing up and down," said Fathia when Safa and I were there with her.

"Did you know, my dad said he was locked up here during the first Intifada," I said. "Now he's behind bars in another prison, an Israeli one this time. There are Palestinian prisons and Israeli prisons, but what's the difference? The prisoners are all Palestinians."

"This place is like a chameleon," said Safa, from the other side of the room. "You can't tell the difference between top and bottom, front and back!"

Fatima laughed. Then she said, "Stop worrying, Philistia. Do what I've done and leave the village behind you."

"And my dad – what would become of him if I left the village behind?" I thought aloud.

One of the prisoners was walking near the fence, shading his eyes with his hand and trying to see something in the distance. When I checked from the side of the balcony to see what he was looking at, I found that it was a shepherd up on the hill with his sheep.

"Grandma, where is the light in this darkness?" I asked myself.

Mum had nothing positive to say when I rang to tell her I was staying with Fathia in Nablus.

"I don't trust you with the girls there!" she grumbled.

This really annoyed me and I showed it – as tends to happen. "You trust me with the naked women at the hammam, but not with Fathia and the girls in her block! Why? What do you know about them?"

I got more and more irritated, while Mum said nothing. That's what she always does. She loves to see me get wound up, so she can show me how she keeps her cool – something I rarely manage. Which is why I rarely win an argument with her.

I tried to justify why I needed to stay over in Nablus. I simply had to, I explained, because of work. I calmed down enough to explain how busy it was going to be at work on Mothers' Day. Every girl and her mother or mother-in-law would be at the hammam, hoping to put their disagreements behind them. Hoping for a fresh start and to come out feeling refreshed.

I tried to sweeten the atmosphere. "How about you and I have some quality time together, Mum?" I suggested.

I heard her laugh down the line.

"Come to the hammam with me. I'll scrub your skin until it gleams. After all, perhaps there'll be a new prisoner release deal and Dad will be let out! You'll need to be ready for him. When he sees you, your skin will be soft and glowing as a newborn baby."

We had often hoped that my father might be released as part of the recent prisoner exchange deal, but it hadn't happened yet. We waited for him to be released in the first round and he wasn't. We didn't lose hope and waited for him in the second round, but he still didn't get out then. And now here I was making fun of the whole thing and turning it into part of a deal with Mum to get her to agree to come for a spa treatment.

"What do you think, Mum?"

As I asked this I remembered Safa once saying, "Nobody knows how Israel thinks!"

"What about us?" I'd asked Safa.

"We don't think!" she'd replied with a laugh.

My mum didn't laugh though. She remained silent. I know what it means when she goes quiet.

She's not happy. I knew then that if it was a question of her having to actively agree to something, she would refuse. And that's exactly what happened: she turned down the invitation to the hammam, but felt obliged to let me stay over with Fathia. So, I basically lied to Mum about work to get my way.

"A white lie," Fathia reassured me later. "Parents don't mind the occasional one. In fact, they thrive on it the more you do it."

It was true that it was a busy week at the hammam, but not so much that it affected the opening hours. The hammam was only open for women two days a week – Sundays and Tuesdays – and the remaining days were for the men. That was why I'd arranged to go to university on Saturdays, Mondays and Wednesdays.

"And the men?" Mum asked, in an attempt to uncover a flaw in my story.

"The hammam's for women only this week. The men can take a bath in the washtub." I tried to turn it into a joke to overcome my guilt at lying. I just wanted to stay away from home a while. For one or two days.

Fathia picked up on that mood and played on it. "Liberate yourself! Open the doors of your life! You're living in the shadows, Philistia. See the city at night. Night in the real world is clearer than day in the world that's in your head."

I wanted that. To see the city with the eyes of the night, not the eyes of the day. After coming here for several months, Nablus wasn't the same as before, I could see that. Not the same as when I used to come here, dragged behind my mum like a goat with a rope around its neck, across mountains, hills, valleys and rivers, the tall palm trees in the centre like an oasis of date palms! An unfamiliar place always seems bigger. The more you get to know a place, the smaller it shrinks until it can fit in your hand. I had been to Nablus before, but coming now was nothing like the whistle-stop visits once or twice a year when I was younger, to buy new clothes for Eid, when people jostled in the *souq* and sweat dripped from Mum's brow and from her armpits, and the heavy black plastic bags dug yellow and bluey-red rings into my fingers – all those impressions that were equally unexpected and equally unpleasant.

So, this was night in Nablus. I flopped down on the bed next to Fathia. Should I tell her what was in my head? She would say I'd gone crazy. It would give her yet more evidence to corroborate her theory. She'd say, "You're a funny one, Philistia. You combine great courage and morbid weakness. Excessive audacity and saintly bashfulness. More secrets of the body are revealed to you than to other girls your age or older, yet the simplest things that girls our age have discovered are hidden from you. You blush and look terrified if a young man speaks to you, and yet you know more than most people about the differences between men's and women's bodies. When you walk down the street, you're all shifty and awkward, contorting all over the place like a bendy dildo that's terrified of bumping into anyone!"

She would stop to see my reaction, then continue. "Yes! Yes, I swear that's right. It's what I've always said, and I stand by it now. In fact, that's not all."

"Er, what else?" I would ask, dumbfounded.

"It's because of your Grandma Zahia and washing all the dead bodies – that world still puts you on edge. That's what's caused you these problems."

"What problems? You haven't even heard what I was going to say!"

"I know you well, Philistia. You're going to start talking about the other world. About the torches with flames carried by cherubs or butterflies, or something. Go on, tell me, isn't that what you were going to say?"

Fathia would sit cross-legged in the middle of the bed, ready to listen.

I'd prop myself up with a pillow, leaning on the headboard of the bed. I'd be feeling flushed despite how cool it was in the room. How did Fathia know what went on in my head? I didn't remember letting her into my world in such detail. Had I really told her all of that? But was she teasing me? That was my world she was talking about – what gave her the right to make fun of it? She had never touched it, or smelled it, or tasted it. She had never heard my world like I had!

"Fathia! Don't make fun of me," I'd say, offended.

Fathia would smile affectionately. "Come on. I want to hear." And she'd say it again when she saw the lack of enthusiasm in my eyes. "Honestly, I want to hear what you have to say!"

Would I tell her about Bayrakdar, the guy who had begun to visit me in my dreams since I started working at the hammam? Should I tell her that I had glimpsed him more than once at Khan al-Wakala in the old town? And that even though I followed him quickly and didn't get sidetracked, even though I followed him straight as a bullet, I still lost sight of him in one of the alleyways.

If I did, she would tease me. She would say, "So, you have this theory that there are two separate worlds?"

I would nod and expand by explaining that I didn't think one world was superior to the other. After all, which one was real? Bayrakdar or Fathia? But I couldn't tell her all this – it would mess with her mind. She definitely wouldn't get it! I decided I wouldn't say anything about it. I would stick to what she could make sense of.

"I was going to tell you about my dreams," I could tell her.

"And what was special about them?" Fathia would ask.

"The dance floor expands with every dream," I'd reply.

"And are there many people dancing?"

"There are more and more all the time."

"Have I ever been there?"

"No, you haven't," I'd say. "You've never stripped off in front of me. You haven't died. And you haven't been born in front of me, for me to sterilise your belly button!"

"I want to be on that dance floor, Philistia."

"Come to the hammam on your day off, then.

You and Fatima and Safa. I'll ask Umm Walid to give you a discount."

"A discount on what, exactly?"

"On the hammam, Fathia."

"And dancing in the water that gushes from the eyes with their lashes, and the waterfall and the waves with the dancing women and the babes … the naked, the deceased, the spinsters, the depressed … the ones who've miscarried, the ones who are misjudged, the happy, the beautiful, the ones who want to be happy and beautiful … all having a dance with your Grandma Zahia hosting the party?"

I'd laugh, and Fathia would wink.

'Free entry, Fathia! Why don't you come and see?"

But no, I decided, *I'm not going to tell you. I won't let you infiltrate my world. Nobody will.*

This world was mine and mine alone, this world I had inhabited since Grandma Zahia first took me with her and taught me the secrets of life and the secrets of death. When she taught me how to prepare a body for burial.

She stretched out her hand and pressed the belly of the dead woman. With a flannel she wiped away the excretions from the woman's nose and from her mouth and from between her thighs. She filled the jug with tepid water and poured it over the body, moving from one part to another. She did that with her eyes watching mine closely. And from time to time she stroked my hair and murmured something. When she had finished she retired to a corner of the room and put her arm around me, and I fell asleep and dreamed the first of my dreams.

I saw the old woman on the wooden chair, slowly, slowly starting to stand up. She ran her hand over her body, looking at my grandma. And when she had confirmed to herself that every limb was in its place, she smiled at my grandma and my grandma smiled back at her. Shuffling to the edge of the chair, the old lady placed first one foot then the other on the floor, then she began to take her first steps like a baby.

"Is she a good woman, Grandma?" I asked.

Grandma replied in a compassionate voice I had never heard her use before, "Who are we to judge people, Philistia?"

The woman approached my grandma and took her hand. Grandma stood up to go with her. Her fingers let go of mine.

"Take me with you!" I screamed.

The old woman moved away and almost disap-peared. Grandma moved away with her and almost disappeared too.

I screamed, "Don't leave me, Grandma!"

Grandma hugged me tightly, and I slept in her arms, breathing in her smell of snuff, and hearing her moist-sounding voice as she prayed for God's protec-tion, chanting over my head, "In the name of Allah, the Merciful, the Compassionate," and reciting the last *suras* of the Qur'an. I slept like I would never sleep again.

4

BAYRAKDAR

This wasn't the first time I'd met Bayrakdar. It wasn't even the second or third. We'd been having these encounters for ages, for so long that I could no longer pinpoint the precise day when I first saw his ghostly image on the wall of the hammam, in the same space where the ghost of Grandma Zahia appears and disappears.

How did we get to know each other all that time ago? Did our souls meet first? Was it because we worked in the same place, at different times in history? Was it the similarity of our lives that brought us together: my dad, imprisoned by the Israeli occupation, and his father who was imprisoned during the British Mandate? Was it the fact that I had been used to seeing women's bodies since my childhood and he had been used to seeing men's bodies since his?

Or was it our unusual names?

"Where's your name from, Bayrakdar?" I asked him.

"It's a Turkish name. It means 'the flag bearer'. It was a name given to my grandfather. He carried the flag when they were fighting the Turks."

"Was he Turkish?"

"He was Palestinian," Bayrakdar replied, and he started to tell me about his grandfather, who as a young man had been strong and courageous. Like many young Palestinians at the time, he had been conscripted into the ranks of the Ottoman army and was forced to run away from his posting in Libya and the intolerable conditions. Half-starved, he fled and managed to cross Egypt. He reached Palestine in three months. Two days after his arrival, the Ottomans captured him and took him back to the army. He ran away again, and again got caught. He was lined up for the same fate as any deserter: the firing squad. But he got there first and shot himself in the foot.

"You didn't get drafted if you were injured," Bayrakdar explained.

"Did he die?" I asked.

"He wasn't afraid of death. He didn't want to remain a starving subject of a regime that oppressed his people and stole their land. My grandfather, like other Palestinians and Arabs, was a subject without rights – all he received were orders and punishments. But that didn't stop my grandfather. Eventually he rallied a group of men who insisted on making him their leader. They gave him the nickname Bayrakdar, as a joke to start with. With time it became my grandfather's official name – both when he was wanted by the Ottoman Turks for the mutinies against them, then later when he fought against the British when they occupied his country.

"My grandfather was killed at the end of the Second World War, before seeing his country Palestine fall into the hands of another occupier. Some said the Turks killed him. But others said he was killed by the English. Meanwhile, others said that he had choked on the noxious fumes of an occupation that was spreading like a pungent toxin. But whatever it was that finished him off," said Bayrakdar, "he remained the flag bearer, and he fell before the flag fell. My father went on to carry the same flag and it got him arrested by the English. He passed it on to me and I brought it with me to the hammam. Now

I pick up my jug to pour water over the shoulders of men who served in the British army!"

"Stand up to them, Bayrakdar," I said.

"Time has passed, Philistia. I'm from the past. But you're from the present." Bayrakdar said this with a touch of sadness in his smile. Then he asked me about my name.

"My dad chose it," I answered. I spoke in a light, humorous tone, trying to chase away his sadness. "I'm not named after my grandma – God rest her soul – but after my country. My dad loved Palestine so much that he called me Philistia, after the first people who lived in this land. It's more common for people to name their daughters Falasteen – the Arabic spelling of Palestine. You come across quite a lot of girls with the name Falasteen, whereas no one has ever heard of the name Philistia, so they can never say it right. Some people call me *Fils*, as in penny, or they turn that into a feminine name, *Filsa*. Others get the letters muddled up altogether and shorten it to *Saltia* or *Salavia*, as though it meant 'Celtic' or 'Slavic'. People seem to love distorting my name, maybe because they think it sounds foreign. Or they tease me by turning it into the name of a vegetable like *fasoulia*, and then they apologise for calling me a green bean, as if I cared enough to get upset about it."

"But wouldn't you be annoyed if you turned into a bean?"

"Or if Palestine turned into a bean."

"So, can a name claim back an occupied country?" asked Bayrakdar, gazing into the distance.

I turned his face back towards me. "A name is a sign that refers to its owner," I said. "The person can disappear, but the name continues to exist. Or the name can vanish, but the person still exists."

I then asked him a question. "If I picked up an axe and chopped something or someone up, would its name be chopped up into little pieces?"

"No."

"But it would feel injured and like its pride was wounded. It would get weaker and eventually waste away."

"May you keep your name for ever," said Bayrakdar with tenderness in his voice.

"And may you keep yours, Bayrakdar," I replied. "Or you could share it with your grandchildren."

We walked – Bayrakdar and I. Nearby were a few trees in their first growth. Taxis were sounding their horns. People walked by. There was a vendor selling popcorn from his wooden cart and someone else was selling books. He had them heaped up on the ground in front of him and was busy arranging them tidily.

"Naked bodies are all alike when you close your eyes," said Bayrakdar. "And block your ears. And open your nose and your sense of touch."

Bayrakdar comes from the world of Grandma Zahia, I thought. Which is he – a message or a light?

"Who taught you the secrets of the body?" I asked him.

"It was handed down from my other grandfather to my mother and me."

"Was he a corpse washer?"

"Yes. He would go from village to village. If someone died, the relatives would say 'Come, O Haj Suleiman,' and he'd get on his donkey and set off for that village to attend to the body."

"Tell me what you learned from him."

"He taught me that the senses must open their ears to receive the message from the body. Each body's soul has a message, which seeks a route to flee the body. If it isn't received by the hands of the corpse washer, then it will drift off into thin air, leaving the corpse beneath your hands just as when it was laid out. The secrets of the soul make themselves understood through the hands. The hands are the eyes of the one who stands over the body, and the body is the mouth of the one who sleeps."

"What do the eyes do if the mouth is closed?"

"My grandfather Suleiman said that for every mouth there was a key."

"And if your hands can't find it?"

"That means they don't understand its language."

"How can the hands learn?"

"My grandfather said that with practice the hands can acquire the keys to the body."

"Can you inherit them?"

"The keys can be neither passed on nor inherited. They pass of their own volition from one who loves to one who is loved."

"So, the keys are secrets that pass to the people who possess them?"

"Or the people go to the secrets."

"How did you come to me?"

"In my sleep."

"Where did you find me?"

"In your sleep."

"And have we met somewhere else before?"

"In our dreams ..."

We walked – Bayrakdar and I. I told him that I would see him in my dream if he didn't appear in reality. I told him that I went to sleep in order to see him. He said he also looked forward to me going to sleep so he could see me. So, I slept, and we walked – Bayrakdar and I. I told him I was afraid of the city and he told me that he didn't know the city, but that I shouldn't be afraid.

"No one knows anything in this country," I told him. "No one has a clue. They're all just sleepwalking." After a pause, I added, "Grandma Zahia knew everything." Then I asked him another question. "Did people know anything in your day?"

"No one knows anything in your day and neither did they in mine, Philistia. If they did, they wouldn't have lost their country." He added, "Perhaps my grandfather Bayrakdar died because he tried to find out."

"The martyrs and the prisoners are trying to make sense of it," I said. After a pause I finished my thought. "But I always thought I knew something – that behind my silence lay my complete knowledge."

"He who enters the hammam is not the same as he

who leaves," he said, quoting the proverb. "And you're the expert, you should know." (Fathia also once said this to me as a joke. I guess we never come back from anywhere the same person as we are before we go.)

"There is no complete knowledge, Bayrakdar. I've started to realise this. University isn't a place of complete knowledge. University is like a bridge to knowledge. And Safa – Miss Know-It-All – she doesn't know anything either. Neither does my mum. She never has any answers when I ask her about Dad, like when will he get out of prison? When will the occupation leave him alone? Or whenever my brother Saeed asks, with his childish innocence, when will Palestine be liberated? She never has any answers. She just says, 'I don't know. There is no truth that we can ever fully know, darling.'"

"And what *is* truth, Philistia?"

"Something we can believe in at any one time and that we can hold in our hands like a body that surrenders completely to our touch."

"And if it doesn't surrender to our touch?"

"We'd make it surrender to us, Bayrakdar."

I then said something that made me feel like that woman who comes to the hammam every month: "You have a funny name, Bayrakdar. What could I turn it into? By radar. Barricade. Barracuda!"

Bayrakdar smiled and asked which one suited him best.

I thought for a moment, playing around with his name. "Buckaroo. Or *barqouq* – plum!"

Bayrakdar laughed and his teeth flashed bright white. He said, "Barqouq and Fasoulia! The plum and the bean. The fruits of two different plant families."

"Well, you're a fruit and I'm a vegetable," I was quick to add, staring unabashedly into his eyes as I spoke.

His face seemed bright, radiant.

Absent-mindedly, I added, "You're a plum I can pluck from the tree with my eyes."

"And my hands?" he asked, taking my hands in his.

"Your hands are your eyes. I see a reflection of myself in them."

He replied in a gentle voice, softer than I'd ever heard, softer even than Grandma Zahia's. "They're a mirror just like yours."

I slept, and we walked – Bayrakdar and I. In my dream I told him, "I know you well, Bayrakdar. Don't leave me on my own. Knowledge is love."

"But you and I live in two different times," he

replied sadly. "Our home is in our imagination."

"Let's plant a garden in our imagination, then," I said. "A garden of fruit and vegetables, with a plum tree and a beanstalk. The beanstalk will climb up the tree, and the plums and the beans will intertwine as they hang down, so no hand or eye can come between me and you."

Bayrakdar laughed and the plum tree was planted in my heart, and from it hung countless ripe *barqouq* plums wrapped in an embrace with endless green and yellow *fasoulia* beans.

5

The PICTURE
FRAME

Dear Dad,

I miss you more than anything in the world. That's what I wanted to tell you most of all.

Now I'll tell you what I've done with the lovely embroidered picture frame you sent me. Do you remember the photo Uncle Hassan took of us at Eid? It was Eid al-Fitr, but I can't remember which year. Do you remember the year? It was definitely Eid al-Fitr, because I remember being so excited I couldn't wait. I had fasted for ten days during Ramadan and you promised to give me five shekels for every day I fasted, so that was five times ten. Fifty shekels! It was the first time in my life I'd ever had so much money. In the picture, Grandma's sitting on the doorstep of the room that's sunny in the morning and you're standing next to me, your back arched like you're trying to look macho, and I'm holding my new doll, the one I called Pistachio. I bought Pistachio for twenty shekels and spent the rest of the money on other things, like a bottle of nail varnish and some socks with frilly tops.

So, just before I started writing you this letter I put the photo from that day in the frame that you gave Mum to give to me two weeks ago. When I look at the picture, I see a handsome young man and an old woman whose face seems to radiate light. And me. My hair was a big frizzy mess, although Mum had given me a bath early that morning and had massaged it with olive oil and pulled it into two bunches with bobbles with little bananas on. I still remember those little bananas, because Nahil always wanted to eat them. But my hair was wild and rebelled against Mum and her bunches. It exercised its right to freedom and stuck out in every direction like the rays of the sun. You can see the rays of sunshine in the picture and you're laughing – your moustache is hovering on its own over your mouth. You're wearing your dark blue denim jacket and light blue jeans. Grandma has a smile on her face, and you and I are laughing, me with my tongue sticking out, and my hand is reaching out of the picture pushing someone to the side, but I can't remember who. Mum said it was Auntie Hoda, and that she wanted to be in our picture but I wouldn't let her.

The picture was supposed to be just of Grandma Zahia. Uncle Hassan told her, "I'm going to get a photo of you, to remember you by." But then you and I ran up and squeezed in next to her. So, it ended up being a photo of the three of us, and now it's in the frame you decorated for me with the colourful embroidery. I can tell you spent ages on it. I remember I once asked you, "How do you spend your long days in prison, Dad?"

And you said, "Time is my needle."

I don't know why but when Mum came back from visiting you and she gave me the frame, and gave some other things to Sawsan, Nahil and Saeed, I immediately thought that it would be perfect for this photo. Mum said, "And this is for Philistia." And straightaway the photo popped into my head. I jumped up to look for it in the photo album. You'll see what I mean when you see it – it's the perfect match. You'll see where you wrote "Little Princess Philistia" and you'll get the feeling that you should have written "Grandma Zahia and a young man with a moustache"!

Little Princess Philistia has grown up, and my wild hair – which Grandma always used to call her "strands of gold" as she breathed in the olive-oil scent – is smoother and tidier now. I went to the salon with Fathia and they made it all sleek and smooth. The hairdresser smeared on this disgusting, stinky conditioner – honestly, it smelled like sewage! Fathia and I had to hold our noses, and we asked the hairdresser where she got it from – was it from Abu Mahmoud's house?

Dad, do you remember that time when Abu Mahmoud's cesspit leaked on to the street? And it stank so bad you could smell it throughout the entire neighbourhood? Remember how Uncle Hassan showed off that he could tell exactly what Abu Mahmoud's family had eaten that day – lentils or chips or maqlooba*? He was trying to convince us that he could tell from the smell, and gradually it became a competition and I joined in. I had learned the secret of smells from Grandma Zahia, but Uncle Hassan didn't know that and he kept saying the opposite of whatever I said. Anyway, that disgusting gloopy stuff, which smelled like Abu Mahmoud's cesspit, felt hot when the hairdresser smeared it on to my hair. And do you know what? When she finished, my hair was smooth but I couldn't help feeling sad – my strands of gold and rays of sunshine were gone.*

Mum said I should have asked your permission first, because you might have not let me go to the salon to have my hair conditioned – as if you'd want my hair to be a wild mess that takes an hour to comb! I told her you wouldn't mind but she kept insisting. I reminded her that you'd agreed when I wanted to get a job at the hammam. Then she said that it hadn't been easy to get you to agree and that she'd asked your cellmate, Abu Hazem, to persuade you. I pointed out to Mum that the fact that you did agree in the end means that you trust me, not that you trust Abu Hazem – because after all, how long have you known Abu Hazem?

Auntie Mariam also had something to say about me getting my hair conditioned, even though her daughters are always going to the salon. She tut-tutted about how I was going to the salon while my dad was in prison – as though it were something shameful! She also disapproved of me getting the job at the hammam, on the grounds that you're in prison. Dad, everyone in the entire village thinks they can poke their nose into our business and have an opinion about everything, just because you're in prison! Dad, what are we supposed to do – just stop living? Stop having fun? Stop doing anything that might make us smile? We never forget you, Dad. We think about you at every good meal, every time one of us smiles, on every cold winter's day. And whenever we need to change the gas cannister or fix the bathroom tap! Or whenever any of us gets sick, or when our sadness outweighs all the reasons we can find to be happy … But we still want to keep on living until you come back.

I told Fathia, "Now I've got hair on my head instead of sunshine." I was running my hands through my hair in front of the big mirror in the living room. "Now my dad won't be able to warm himself on its rays."

Do you remember, Dad, when you used to tug my hair in the winter and say, "Come on, sunshine, warm me up!"?

I was thinking about it again at the hammam today. What's scary, I thought, is that they're nothing more than naked women! Is it because they're alive? What's the difference between life and death for a naked woman, stretched out with her eyes closed? In both cases, they are women who surrender to my hands. In both cases, my hands have to be compassionate.

"Be kind, meek, modest," Grandma once instructed me. "Be blind, deaf and dumb."

"And what else, Grandma? Tell me."

"Give me your hands, Philistia. Stand behind me and move your hands with mine." Grandma's hands moved as she spoke and with them my hands slid over the naked body, starting at the head. "The hair is a leafy canopy, the branches of a tree of passion. The head is a gift from God. The eyelids are the shutters of the windows on to life. The nose is a balcony where the breeze blows through. The mouth is a treasure trove of pearls. The neck is a support for the soul. The shoulders are each the seat of a throne. The breastbone is the tree trunk from which the soul's branches stem. The breasts are flowers of milk. The navel is the source of a spring. The crotch is the core of a pear that bears its seeds within. The thighs are two pitchers. The spine is the measuring tape of creation. The feet are the slippers of life."

"How can I remember all this, Grandma?" I whispered.

"Don't try and remember it, Philistia, just sing it," she whispered. "You're not in an exam, remember? It's a dance."

I whispered to Grandma, "Can dead people dance?"

"Their souls dance," she whispered. "Their bodies remain with us, the living, until they're buried. Then they belong to the world above."

"Who looks after them up there?"

Grandma came closer to whisper in my ear, and I heard her warm laughter coming from a hidden world. "That knowledge is with God – he who granted them life and planned their fate."

Dear Dad,

Hello again. It's evening and I've sat down on my bed to carry on with my letter to you. I got back from Nablus about four hours ago. I had dinner then slept for about an hour and a half. We had cooked white beans today – fasoulia. You know how I've never liked beans? White or green or yellow? Well, now I do. Before Saeed, Sawsan or Nahil could tease me, I

laughed first and cracked the old joke myself. "Mmmm, we're
having me *for dinner. That's my body, that's my leg ...*" *and
I picked out the beans from the sauce. Mum glared at me. She
was just trying to stop us from fighting so we could eat dinner
in peace, but it meant telling me off as usual.*

"If one of them had called you that you'd be furious, and
here you are reminding them. You've only got yourself to blame."

"That means I've grown up then, Mum."

*It's true, Dad – I have grown up. I don't get wound up by
them like I used to, and I've even started to quite like my nickname* Fasoulia. *So I've gone back to the old game of thinking
up silly new names for my friends: Fatima is now* Tomato,
Safa's Saffron *and Fathia's* Fattoush. *And altogether we're
the Mezze Crew.*

*Sometimes when Grandma Zahia was wrapping up a
newborn baby, she used to ask me,* "What shall we call him,
Philistia?" *So I'd come up with a name for him, after staring
at him for a while with narrowed eyes. But my suggestions
didn't always go down well with the family. They would
already have a number of choices, and now here I was adding
another name to the mix, and who was I anyway? The
granddaughter of Hajja Zahia, who snipped the cord, tied
up the belly button, washed and wrapped up the baby. But
who was I really? Someone whose name no one can remember or say properly. What would their response be? They'd*

mutter something, then ask what made me think of the name
I'd suggested.

"*Why did you suggest* Rafiqa *– 'companion'?*"
they'd ask.

"*So she would have friends,*" *I'd say.*

"*Why the name* Alia *– 'high'?*"

"*Because no one is as high as the stars in the sky.*"

"*Why* Itra *– 'sweet scent'?*"

"*Because nothing is lovelier about a rose than its scent.*"

But Mum once asked me, "*Why did you choose the name*
Sawsan for your sister?"

"*I don't know,*" *I replied.*

Do you remember, Dad? The first person I ever chose a
name for was Sawsan, and I didn't know why at the time. If
you didn't already have a name, Dad, I'd choose one for you.
Do you know what it would be? I don't think you'll have heard
it before: Bayrakdar. *Do you know what it means? No? Shall*
I tell you how to find out? Find a prisoner in jail with you
whose dad absconded from the Ottoman army on the Libyan
front. Ask him.

At the hammam today, Umm Walid patted me on
the shoulder.

"Well done, Philistia. Your mother said you
wouldn't let me down and she was right."

She held out a white towel and draped it over my shoulder. She handed me some Nabulsi soap and a piece of loofah.

"Give this to the guest and take her to that room," she said, pointing to one of the three small rooms, "and wash her body with soap and water." There were two rooms on the right and the third was on the left.

Grandma was looking down at me from behind the woman: a pale ghostly image appeared on the wall above the large tiles that the water splashes against. My hands were dripping with water, and as my plastic flip-flops slapped against the floor, the water squelched making a croaking sound like a frog.

Dear Dad,

I'm back. It's a quarter past midnight. I was waiting for Nahil to go to sleep before I carried on writing to you, because although Nahil doesn't poke her nose into my business like Sawsan does, I still feel a bit embarrassed writing to you if I know she's awake. She's asleep now, and as tomorrow is my day off I feel like I can stay up chatting to you. I cherish this freedom at night and I miss it during the day. I want to tell you that whenever I walk into the hammam, I sense you there with me – it's as humid as the sea air where you are. The sea. You said before that you can hear its roar and see its waves, but you can't touch it. The water. In your dreams you're touching that water that you can't reach, and here it is every day in my hands.

I didn't choose to work at the baths so that I could be close to you, close to your world, but so that I could be — as Fathia put it — closer to my dreams and my childhood. Do you know what I feel when I'm at the hammam, Dad? I feel like my senses stop working. Like they switch off. My ears are no longer ears, my eyes are no longer eyes, my hands are not hands, my nose is not a nose. When I arrive at work, I tell myself I'm throwing off my senses now. Getting rid of myself. I toss my senses over my shoulder like I'm throwing myself away, so I can sleepwalk through my dream.

This is my dream, Dad. You're in it with me. The high walls. The humid air that is so dense you can barely breathe. Your instructions come from afar, you hear them and you can't hear them, you do as they say, as though you can hear nothing else. Bodies pass by your mat. Over the hot tiled floor. Among the bodies, you hear talking again, so you push it away and vanish inside yourself. You tune in only to yourself and set off sleepwalking. You're dreaming and you see me. Hot, sweaty Philistia, her body warm, her dead skin peeling off and regenerating, while more and more of your cells age and die.

A young man and a girl walk in a dream — their roles reversed. In our dreams, you and I, we're close to the sea but we *can't touch it. The smell of the water hits you in the back of the throat. The hammam ceiling is studded with tiny dots of light. They gather on the ceiling and you keep dreaming they're going to fall, but they don't fall. How many times have you fallen over in your dream, Dad? How many times have you been tripped over, surprised by the sound of the sea in your ears? Your hands and your feet are shackled, and you shout, "I want to bathe in the sea!"*

The water rushes over me and I dive in. The longer the night stretches on – and the world is one long night – the deeper I walk and the deeper you walk. You are in the darkness of your dream and I am in the darkness of my dream. Who can see the other's path? You who chose it or I who followed you and lost you? Is it your darkness or mine?

Fathia said that my job is so perfect for me, it's made to measure. Yes, it is perfect. If I'd got a job in a clothing store, how would Grandma Zahia come and see me? Where would Bayrakdar appear? The hammam extends the time I spend asleep. Did I always love sleeping, Dad?

This is you and me. A father and a daughter all alone. In a photo in a frame decorated with threads of colours sewn with the needle of time. If it weren't for the light that radiates among us, we would be surrounded by darkness by now, our flames burned out. What did you do, Dad, to have your time stolen away so far from us? Did I walk all that way for these damp, dripping walls to steal my time? For my life to be taken over by naked bodies. By this memory I've inherited. For my senses to be absent.

So I walk and walk. Every day I walk in my dreams. I reach out with my hand. I see hands in the distance, dissolving into the wall of the hammam. Your hands. Grandma's hands. Bayrakdar's hands. But I can't see the hands of Fathia or Safa or Fatima. As though I'm not a child of my generation. I belong to a previous generation, and I'm living out the rest of a life that was mine but which has somehow vanished, leaving a void in time. And now I'm a girl who emerges from the wall, reaching out into life to play in that void.

Dad, is there life outside the hammam too? I sometimes wonder. I think the whole world is one big hammam, where our senses are suspended. Everyone around me sees but doesn't see. Everyone is running through life carrying their lamp or their torch, and some don't realise that they're running with this light in their hand, or that the wind has blown out the flame, or that their hands are empty, or that the lamp is broken and all they have left in their hand is the handle.

Dad, I miss Grandma Zahia.

6

WHERE ELSE *can a* TREE GROW?

That night, our village Deir Sabra was broken, like a branch clinging on to its tree by a scrap of bark, where what remains of the water of life trickles out like a tear trying not to fall. The soldiers cut down hundreds of olive trees on the edge of our village. No one could stop them, no matter how they tried. Not the women who hugged the trees trying to keep them from harm. Not the children playing in front of the bulldozers with broken sticks. They carried on playing as though they thought they were in a cartoon and ended up getting hurt. Not the teens and young men carrying axes and sticks who took on the soldiers, their tears flowing like rivers, and who came away filthy from the smoke, the dusty soil and their own blood.

That evening, after the battle, Fathia and I sat in the shade of our tree, looking down on the destruction from afar, trying in vain to ignore our grief. Fathia's hand was wrapped in a blue rag where she had cut herself. Earlier she had fallen to the ground as the smoke rose over our heads and a broken tree trunk fell on her hand.

"You know what?" she said. "When I heard the shooting, I almost ran off and left my hand behind under that tree trunk."

"Life wanted to write another chapter for you. It'd be called 'Fathia, the One-handed'," I said, trying to sound wise.

"More like 'Fathia, the Half-hearted'," she said, and then she fell silent. She was still leaning against the trunk of the big tree in the village, the lovely shady one, staring at the ground and playing with the soil.

"What if they cut down our shady tree too? Then what would you lean your back against?"

"Never mind my back," she replied, scratching the word "back" in the soil with a twig. "The tree will be just a cut-off stump, and when its branches dry out an Israeli will have a fire to warm himself up. Good for him. So the whole tree-felling operation will have been well worth it."

"Are you talking about victory?"

"No, not at all. I was talking about defeat."

"You don't seem very upset," I said, as though I wanted to provoke her.

"What do you want me to do? Climb up the tree and throw myself out of it? The only thing I'd achieve would be to break my legs, and they're no use for making a nice warm fire."

"Just think, Fathia. Here we are sitting under the shady tree, just like when we were two carefree little girls, when we used to play here then run home dripping with sweat or water."

"Yeah, we've grown up a lot," said Fathia. "If I asked you how many times you've been hurt, you wouldn't be able to count."

"I've only been hurt once," I said. "But it's a wound that spans my entire body. It stretches from top to bottom like my spine. I can't walk without it, I'd fall over without it…"

"If your whole body were covered in little scratches, you'd need a map so huge you'd need eight octopus arms to carry it."

"Why have we suddenly grown up so much, Fathia?"

"Because we started to make sense of things early. I mean we learned about a lot of things that don't make any sense."

"I think you're miserable because they didn't publish your poem in the newspaper," I said.

"I'd be even more miserable if they had," she replied.

"Now who doesn't make any sense?"

Fathia burst into tears. She hugged me and cried. I didn't say anything to her, or perhaps I was saying it silently, "Cry, Fathia, cry. That's what we wanted to do from the start."

In front of us, in the distance, was a landscape of hacked-down olive trees and heaps of soil like tiny red hills and small people like magical creatures scrabbling about inspecting the damage. There was all of this and Fathia was hugging me and crying. An image popped into my mind: a swollen stomach, cracked with stretch marks. That woman who asked me to scrub her over and over until I rubbed away those lines on her skin. The image of her inflated belly sat in my mind like a rubber beach ball blown up so tight it was close to bursting. But all this didn't stop Bayrakdar's radiant face from smiling like one final remaining spot of joy amid all the arid wastelands. As I remembered the plum tree growing in my heart, the swollen, cracked beach ball stomach disappeared from my mind. I wiped away the tears that had started to flow. My voice crept up through my body to emerge in the form of words.

"What do you say? Time for a snack? Fancy some *fasoulia* beans?" I suggested.

Fathia laughed and nodded. I shook into her hand a few white beans we'd brought with us after picking them out of Mum's stew. She had made it with chicken and puréed tomatoes especially for Fathia. When Mum put the casserole dish on the table, she said, "With fresh tomatoes especially for you."

Fathia stayed at mine that night and we slept side by side, Fathia on the right and me on the left, where my sister Nahil usually sleeps. All that sadness put us in a serious mood, perfect for sharing secrets. It had been two months since we had spent so much time talking. We had met a few times and had a brief chat now and then, like when we swapped our pen caps for good luck before exams, and the occasional quick chat about incidents involving naked women, good-looking students, boring teachers and nagging parents. What we hadn't had the chance to talk about were the secrets growing in our hearts, inside each of us. Somehow, we both knew that the other also had a secret that had begun as a seed, then sprouted and grown sprawling stems – each without the other seeing it.

"Tell me about the tree that's been growing in your heart," I asked Fathia.

She told me about the seedling that had with-ered before it had even become a plant. I knew that his name was Ali, but I didn't know that all those poems she had written were for him. In fact, he was her inspiration for taking up writing in the first place. Why do we do this? Perhaps because we only bring our dreams into focus for the sake of those we love.

"You've been dreaming of him and now you have to learn to dream of yourself, of Fathia," I said. "For your love to continue, you need to put your dream away somewhere for the time being. And one day the time will come when that old dream will come true."

"Love doesn't listen to advice, Philistia."

"I know your inspiration is all dry and withered, but would you give up writing and doing all the things you do just because of Ali?"

"He's gone away."

"God be with him. But the important thing is what has he taken with him?"

"He's my first love."

"When you say first love, what do you mean? Think about it," I said, in a light-hearted way, gently tugging a thread on Fathia's jumper.

Fathia closed her eyes and when she spoke it was as though she were asleep. "I mean the first heart your heart throbs for, and the first scent your nose is aware of, the first laughter that makes your eyes laugh too, the first hand that touches your hand, and the first disaster that grabs you by the neck and drags you across the ground and the bumpy roots of the trees."

Then she got up abruptly and pulled her laptop out of her bag. "I'll show you a picture of him," she said with such joy that it almost seemed like the sadness and gloom a moment ago had all been an act.

We looked at his profile picture. We studied it. We checked how many times the post had been shared and how many likes that picture had got, never mind all the other pictures. He was standing on his own in the 'Kit-Kat courtyard' in the middle of the old building of An-Najah University. He had his back to the main library. He wore glasses that made his intelligent eyes lure in anyone whose eyes fell on him, and he had a smile that beamed confidence.

When I saw how good-looking he was I realised my task of making Fathia feel better was going to be challenging. It was even more challenging when I considered how self-assured he was; you could tell from his posture and his offhand responses to a torrent of praise from a stream of beautiful girls.

I decided I needed to find another way to help soothe my friend's bruised soul, after being brushed aside by this handsome, self-confident young man who wouldn't have any trouble finding another girl when he was ready to fall in love. But the method I thought of seemed complicated and not necessarily reliable.

"Leaving you doesn't mean he doesn't love you. And just because he's gone it doesn't mean you can't plant him in your heart. I don't think you should hate him and yank his tree out of the ground. Instead, how about you replant it in the garden at the very back of your soul? So it can grow there for the rest of your life without you being aware of its presence. You won't need to water it; in fact, it will quench your thirst. Many people we love are planted there at the end of the garden, including our loved ones who have died – that's what Grandma Zahia says.

"And do you know what?" I continued. "Look!" I pointed to the screen, circling my finger over his picture. "His body is nothing like your body. Look: you're small and slender, he's tall and chunky. Bodies need to love each other just as much as souls do, and I don't think there was genuine romance between your bodies."

Fathia laughed, laughing and crying at the same time, her tears mingling with the stream from her nose, her lips pursed, and I realised that I had pretty much failed in my attempt to cheer her up. But I didn't despair. I wanted to tell her that my story was more painful, but I knew nobody would understand it, not even Fathia. And then a stray sentence emerged from my mouth.

"At least you have a picture of him, I have nothing!"

Fathia stopped crying, and I almost regretted what I'd said. There was still room to retreat when she asked, "Who are you talking about?"

I tossed out his name quickly like I was throwing a burning ember from my hand: "Bayrakdar."

So, then I finally had to tell Fathia about the guy who constantly visits me in my sleep.

I was ready for her to reply with a loud and clear, "Philistia, you're nuts." But no. Fathia's face didn't give anything away. She pulled out a piece of paper and a pen from her bag. Her voice soft and humble, she said, "Draw a picture of him."

So, I found myself holding a blue ink pen, my hand trembling as I tried to draw a portrait of Bayrakdar. It was the first time it had occurred to me that this man who dwelled in my dreams had the right to have his portrait drawn so I could keep it.

So, I tried, but I failed miserably. I kept trying to draw him, but when I realised I couldn't, Fathia – who was so excited to see what Bayrakdar looked like – had an inspired idea. We looked online and found photos of men, young and old, from all over the world, and I picked out Bayrakdar's features from the faces of men from Niger, Spain, North Korea, Morocco and Brazil: actors, singers, poets and ordinary people, dead and alive.

I stopped at one picture. "There. His eyes are a bit like Bayrakdar's," I said. "His nose is like Bayrakdar's. His smile … if it were a bit less expressive, it would be like Bayrakdar's. His physique reminds me a bit of Bayrakdar, if you changed it just a little bit."

What if I spotted him walking in front of me through the alleys of the internet? If Bayrakdar were a real living person like Ali, he might discover that his love for me wasn't real. He might suddenly decide to leave me and set off travelling abroad, to Germany or Japan, and I would be devastated just like Fathia.

Suddenly I found myself crying. I have to admit that Fathia had a much harder job trying to make me feel better than I had had with her. She cried with me, then laughed as she hugged me tight. She slapped me on the face a few times and said, "Don't be silly! He's just a boy in your dreams, you daft thing! He's not even real!"

"Where do you plant trees for people who aren't here?" I asked. "For absentees?"

"Your Grandma Zahia would say plant them alongside those who are with us," replied Fathia with a seriousness she seemed to summon up out of fear for my bruised soul. "If they've left you," she added, "then their place is at the bottom of the garden, and if they haven't left you then plant a tree for them in the garden of your heart."

"I've planted a plum tree for him in my heart," I replied with a sob, and the stream from my nose was mixed with my tears.

"I'll give you a plum tree that you can plant in the garden," Fathia promised, giving me a pat on the shoulder.

"Really?" I asked, with no actual desire to be sure of anything.

Fathia promised. She swore she'd find me a plum tree that I could plant in the garden by the house.

I pulled the blanket up and wrapped it around me before collapsing back on to the bed. I suddenly felt weak. "I feel ill," I said.

Fathia wrapped another blanket around me with a theatrical air, assuming I was joking. Then she sat down beside me and reached her hand to touch my forehead. "You're fine," she said. "What you need is a poem for Bayrakdar by the great poet Fathia."

Then she started to dictate her verse aloud as she typed:

O sleeping boy from my dreams,
I'm searching for you in the dark.
Until I find you again you'll have
To grow in the garden of my heart.

I see your smile, I hear your laugh –
They give me strength when I'm blue.
O sleeping boy of my dreams,
Will you wake up, so I can too?

Tell me just once if you feel the same,
But don't take forever 'til you do.
Let my hand reach and find your hand,
And say, "I can't live without you."

Fathia didn't forget about Bayrakdar after that, but she didn't tease me like I thought she would. She viewed my predicament with the same gravity as she did her own with Ali.

"If Bayrakdar doesn't intend to abandon you like Ali abandoned me," she said one day, "then he'll have to find a way to become real, more real than just a guy who visits you in your dreams."

I might almost have started to resent Bayrakdar after that, if he hadn't visited me that night and told me, when I told him what Fathia had said, that the same words could apply to me. If I didn't want to abandon him, he said, I needed to live in the dream world instead of in real life, to become the not-real Philistia. I replied without even stopping to think that I couldn't abandon Nahil, Saeed, Sawsan, my mum and all the naked women at the hammam.

"And who would wash the poor dead women in Deir Sabra?" I asked. "Who would cut the umbilical cords of the new babies who arrive day after day into this world?"

I told him that I followed in Grandma Zahia's footsteps and I would do until the day I died.

This made Bayrakdar feel less bad about me not being able to join him. And he reassured me again that no one, not even the Israeli occupiers, would be able to demolish our house as long as it was built in our imaginations.

7

a LONG DREAM

I distinctly remember the first day Grandma Zahia took me with her to work. It was the day Sawsan was born: 25 December 2000, according to her birth certificate. Mum was in terrible pain for several days before the birth, and she was already a few days past the due date. The nurse at the village clinic said that a home birth could endanger her life and that he couldn't be responsible for the delivery.

"Take her to Rafid State Hospital," said the nurse, speaking like he was giving an order.

Dad asked him if he could help them get an ambulance, but the man said he was sorry and then he said, "Don't you know what's going on in the world?" like he was telling Dad off.

Was Mum going to die because Dad didn't know what was going on in the world? What did the world have to do with it? My mum was all that mattered. She was my world. I hated the nurse for saying that and wanted to tell him so. But Dad pulled me by the hand and we got in the car to go home.

On the way, I heard them say that the baby was the wrong way up inside Mum's womb. But Grandma, as so often, knew what needed to be done. Grandma Zahia knew everything really, so for any problem she could always find a solution. She told Mum to bide her time. And she told her she needed to keep moving. But our house, because it's basically just two rooms, didn't give her a lot of space to walk around. She had little choice but to go for a walk on the edge of the village on roads she would never normally set foot on, just to stay out of sight of the nosy neighbours. It didn't take much to set the people of Deir Sabra off gossiping.

"Goodness me, have you seen this? Fadl's wife is out for a stroll while she's in labour! What is the world coming to?"

"Well, we've seen it all now! She's out walking in the rain and her baby's about to pop!"

But nothing was going to stand in Mum's way. As she said, pressing her fingers into her back, no one knew the pain someone else was going through. Trying to give her courage, Dad got ready to go out with her: a clear and unmistakable violation of village customs, which forbade a man and his wife from walking together in public, whether for the sake of enjoyment, or even for the sake of alleviating pain, temporary depression or shifting a baby's position in its mother's womb. In our village, if a man and his wife ever went out to the fields together, the husband was supposed to walk a few metres ahead of her, while she had to resist the temptation to catch up with him – a wish that never once came true in a woman's life. That day, Dad, Mum and I ushered in a new era in the history of walking in our village, but we opted for a back street, slightly further from prying eyes.

It was very cold that day. Mum wrapped a colour- ful woollen shawl around her shoulders and dressed me in my red jacket. It had a hood. I was always impa- tient waiting for winter to come from one year to the next, so that it would rain and I could put my hood up. My red jacket had a plastic outer layer and when the rain fell on it, it sounded like the raindrops on the zinc roofs of the houses. It had a furry layer inside, which I loved in winter. On bitterly cold days, I'd lay it out to sit on and the plastic would rustle whenever

I moved. That magical raincoat was the first and the last present I ever received from Uncle Hassan. He brought it back when he was working in Israel and I heard Mum once telling my aunt that Uncle Hassan had got it second-hand. It was a while before I learned what that meant, but even when I did, it didn't make me love the jacket any less, even though it meant an Israeli girl might have worn it before me. But when it started to rain that day, neither that magic jacket nor anything else could protect us from the rain shower, not even the shady tree, despite its great size and its dense branches stretching in every direction. Rather than sheltering us from the rain, in fact streams of water gushed down from the branches and from the leaves to drench us.

The little walk didn't even help, because in the end Mum and Dad were forced to do exactly what they'd hoped to avoid: cross the checkpoint between our village and Nablus, from where they had heard worrying news of killings, arrests, raids and curfews. Dad spoke about what was happening in Nablus and other places, expressing himself differently to how the nurse had.

"It's like the end of the world out there," said Grandma.

I pictured the world as a tumultuous sea of crashing waves and emerging from the water was a monstrous fish with human legs and heads dangling from its blood-coloured fangs. It was a scene I had seen on television once and although I put my hands over my eyes, through my fingers I could still see the sea, which I had never seen in real life, with its waves crashing. Now I knew that was what the world was like and I was going to keep my hands firmly over my eyes for as long as I could.

It was Sunday evening, and there was Dad with his arm around Mum. She leaned on him as they both got into Abdullah's taxi and vanished behind the shady tree and then the olive grove, the houses and the hills.

The last things I saw of Mum before they drove away were her colourful shawl and her tears as she looked back at me through the window. And when she saw my tears she asked me what I wanted to call the baby girl – I didn't know why Mum had decided that the baby was a girl.

"Sawsan," I replied without giving it any thought.

I didn't know anyone with that name, and I don't remember now where I had heard it. I was thinking of Mum's tearful eyes and mine as they filled up with tears until I could no longer see. My eyes were like a car window with a bucket of water poured over it. Mum reached out her hand to wipe my eyes and it was like the car window winding down.

In between sobs, I added, "And Saeed if it's a boy."

It's Bayrakdar – I recognise his smell, his smile, his eyes, his nose and his whole body. That's him without me needing to tweak anything or change him to make him resemble someone else's picture. I found him waiting for me at the first onion stall, near the fishmonger's. He reached out to take my hand and we started walking together. Now my small hand was in his small hand. This had to be real, or else how could I feel all this happiness that I had never felt before? How was it possible for someone to *seem* so real and for you to believe that he was the happiness you so longed for, when you and he both knew full well that you were both imaginary, that you're walking in your sleep? It was a reality that wrote its own script, and there was nothing we could do but believe in it, even if it contradicted all standard measures of what was real.

Bayrakdar and I were real as far as we were concerned. We were a world for us alone. A life for us alone. Everyone who passed by was busy with their own affairs. They were immersed in their other world. Haggling with vendors over the price of cinnamon, local flowers, Persian narghile tobacco, Hebron vine leaves, antique tea trays, date paste, carob molasses, traditional hummus, cheap children's clothing, wooden walking sticks, more local flowers, and even more local flowers, and cabbages. It all meant nothing to us. None of it mattered to us, to Bayrakdar and me.

"Let's stop a second," I said to Bayrakdar, as we slipped across a side street into the alley that led to the hammam. "I want to get some pumpkin *zalabia*."

"Two, please," we said to the young man.

"My pleasure," he replied, with a smile that flooded his face, and pointed to his eyes as he added the idiomatic reply, "from my eye."

He broke off a piece from the lump of dough on the tray and moulded it into a pyramid. Then he tossed it with a flourish into a large frying pan of oil and, after pressing a second piece into a pyramid, he tossed that in with the first one.

The pyramid-shaped fritters sat side by side on the tray as the vendor pressed shredded pumpkin into the middle, then turned them over as he drizzled them with syrup.

We walked, Bayrakdar and I.

My small hand was in his small hand.

For the first time this street in the centre of the old town smelled of life. I always felt afraid whenever I walked down here on my own. I used to feel like I was walking over the bodies of dead people and could sense their smell wafting by my nose. Sometimes they would tug at my clothes, wanting to stop me in my tracks for some reason. Ghosts and invisible spirits would drift all around me, above me, under my feet. But today, here I was walking along inside the smell and I reached my hand out from amid it as I took the *zalabia* from the vendor's hand. I wonder what my hand looked like to him?

We ate our *zalabia*, Bayrakdar and I. Could he see us, I wonder?

I went into the hammam. The young man behind the wooden screen saw me and didn't see me. He smiled at me as I popped the last bite of *zalabia* into my mouth. Bayrakdar was at my side, I was still sure of it. His small hand was in my small hand. The young man behind the wooden screen looked at Bayrakdar and smiled. Bayrakdar took another nibble of his *zalabia*.

I told the young man I was Philistia and that Bayrakdar had come with me to count the *qamriyat*, the tiny shafts of light that dot the ceiling. The young man smiled. I told him Bayrakdar was usually just a ghost, that he lived here – the hammam was his home. And I told him I was usually a real girl who worked at the hammam, who scrubbed women's bodies with my black mitt that's a bit bigger than my palm and washed them with Nabulsi soap and rinsed them with warm water. The young man smiled. Bayrakdar told him not to worry if we didn't come back out through the door, because we might jump from the roof. We might fly. We might pass through the wall like he sometimes did. The young man smiled and reached out to touch our little hands to check something. His hands were warm and our hands were warm.

When we were inside, Umm Walid came to meet me.

"Why are you late?" she asked.

I told her I'd been eating *zalabia* from the market. Umm Walid smiled and asked me to change and put on my hammam clothes. There were three women waiting in the steam room for me.

I told her I needed to go upstairs first. "I'm just

going to count the shafts of light in the ceiling," I told Umm Walid.

"And get the towels from the line, Philistia," she said.

I nodded. I was still holding hands with Bayrakdar. He pulled me behind him and we slipped away up the narrow staircase, him in front and me following.

"Sit down, my sweetheart," Bayrakdar said. "I'll count the *qamriyat* in the ceiling and get the towels. You just watch and see how Barqouq does it."

So I sat down and watched Barqouq. I could hear Umm Walid calling me. She called to me over and over, while the whole time I sat upstairs watching Barqouq take the towels off the line and check the tiny windows that dotted the ceiling, giving them a wipe to let the light shine through.

Over and over, I called back with the same reply. "OK, Umm Walid," I called down to her. "I'm coming! I've just got a long dream I want to finish."

THE END